A DARK FANTASY ROMANCE

THE HOUSE WINS

APOCALYPTIC FRIENDS TO LOVERS

A.L. SECORD

THE HOUSE WINS:

APOCALYPTIC FRIENDS TO LOVERS

A DARK FANTASY ROMANCE

WRITTEN BY: A.L. SECORD

DARK FANTASY WEREWOLF MAGIC PUBLISHING

THE HOUSE WINS: APOCALYPTIC FRIENDS TO LOVERS
A DARK FANTASY ROMANCE
Copyright © 2025 by A.L. SECORD

Thank you to my friends and my Sullivan and McEwen family that love and support me. A Big Thank you to: God; Trinity and Tori Secord; Andrey Trushin; Theresa McEwen, Brad Sullivan; Ellen Sullivan; David Fox; Shelley Druet; Annie and Jim Bishop, and Kent and Megs Garlough. Thank you to my fans from all of my heart and soul.

DARK FANTASY WEREWOLF MAGIC PUBLISHING Copyright © 2025
This book is available in eBook, and print formats.

Edited by: APRIL SECORD
Book Cover design by: APRIL SECORD

EBOOK ISBN: 978-1-998151-14-1
PAPERBACK ISBN: 978-1-998151-15-8
HARDCOVER ISBN: 978-1-998151-16-5

First Edition: MAY 2025
10 9 8 7 6 5 4 3 2 1

CHAPTER 1

THE FIRST TIME

I remember the way his blonde hair shimmered in the sunlight as he politely asked me to pass him a book from the library shelf. Just hearing his voice was deep and enchanting. I don't know why he had even chosen to speak to me that day, other than what I know now.

My dull, blonde hair was a mess and I was dressed like a slob. I was so pre-occupied with the same book on grief that he had asked me to pass him; that I almost didn't hear him the first time he spoke. When our eyes met I noticed the flash of red and heard him gently tap his foot.

As soon as I met his calm anger I was speechless. He was the most handsome man I had ever seen and I lingered in holding the book with my mouth slightly gaped open. Even though he wasn't amused I smiled and his cheeks turned a dark red. He gently tugged the book from my hand as words seemed to be failing my tongue.

My thoughts were of introduction and pleasantries. But no noise parted my dry lips. When his fingers caressed my hand I exhaled deeply. His skin felt tough and electric. His eyebrows crinkled but he gave me a nod in thanks and then turned to leave. But before this Adonis of a man could escape I had to say something. My soul urged me to speak to him.

"Sir that book is good. But friendship is better." I smiled and called out and he stopped in his gloomy tracks.

"I have neither the time nor the warmth for friendship in my line of work." He said but turned around and stood there gazing at me with these heavenly golden eyes.

"Maybe there is an exception to every rule then. I'm not sure what you are going through but maybe we could go through it together. My name is Julia. I come here to read at that little private booth every Wednesday. You are always welcome to join me. It would be nice to have a friend for the end of the world." I said and extended my hand as he stepped towards me taking my hand gently.

"You can call me Morning Star. I travel a lot for business but I can keep a schedule as long as you can dress for the occasion. A friend during the end of the world is always nice." His voice sounded like church bells so sweet I was on cloud nine as he flashed me his beautiful fanged smile.

Before he left me still gazing after his beauty he paused and turned to me asking ever so deeply and sweetly; "I don't suppose you know how to play poker Julia?"

"Actually I've never played before, but I could learn if you teach me." I said sheepishly with a large grin.

"Yes, I think I would like that immeasurably." His voice seemed so silvery I now felt the blush sweep across my face.

It was from that moment on that we started meeting up at the library on Wednesdays. Then within weeks I was a bigger part of his inner world and he was a bigger part of mine. Even when I dreamt at night, he would be there and then we would have adventures in the dream realm. He became my angel and guardian. We became the closest of best friends humanly possible for the last seven years, of the existence of earth.

Except he isn't human. And secretly I think I fell for him in the very first moment he spoke to me. Under normal circumstances I would just bury these new discovered feelings of intimacy and longing for his affection, but the world is ending tomorrow. If I don't gather the courage to tell him, then I never will. I guess.

🌾🌾🌾🌾

CHAPTER 2

ASTEROID

There is no escape. The Big G. is aiming his fireballs directly at my best friend's temple. He knows we'll be in there exactly when the asteroid hits. He knows everything. He is of course God.

Some of us will be coming here because there is just no point in running. Others are here because they can't leave. Others are coming because they came to the inevitable conclusion. The great reset was bound to happen. I was here because of my contract and because I couldn't help but want to hold my best friends hand at the end of the world.

My contract was a sweet deal. All it took was a little blood. I had the house, the car, and the life. All of which the husband took; set fire to; and then trashed my reputation. Hey what can I say? It was high and fast times. And I was over it. So why not hang out with the grand magician who had become my best friend. I mean we all have to go sometime.

Nothing mattered anymore. My light was only bright because of him. And if he is being wiped from this earth so shall I. I love him. He's my best friend and I can't imagine a world without him in it.

☙☙☙☙

Let's rewind a bit shall we. My name is Julia. My last name is Black but it is all inconsequential, as is everything, except the all night poker game that shall happen this evening until dawn. I think he knows I'm a horrible cheat though. It's a good thing the actual game is loaded and everybody cheats that sits at this table. Maybe it was a pre-requisite or a bonus trait of all the gangly, unruly characters that will be there tonight. I am glad my best friend likes us all anyway.

His big red eyes have this special glow. It's like the light of the Divine is always turned on inside him. A lot of people notice his unearthly beauty when they first meet him. But if he really trusts and cares about you; you will see his true nature. You will see his fanged smile and his big black horns. His muscular form is from years of hard labor despite what humans think. When he fell from heaven it took quite a lot to get this temple cave into shape and a livable standard for all the other fallen angels. And hell hasn't exactly been easy to care for, with all the rift-rafts and cryptids.

☙☙☙☙

Back to the end. So where am I going on the last night of the end of the world? I purchased my one way ticket to Canada's Algonquin Provincial Park. There was a secret pyramid hidden around Canoe Lake and this was the secret location for the grand entrance to his temple.

THE HOUSE WINS: APOCALYPTIC FRIENDS TO LOVERS

The last sealed door opened for me just like it had in all my reincarnations. In the end times I was beginning to remember all of my lives. I remembered being here with him. I slowly made my way through the temple pillars. The cave seemed so empty except the crimson candles that were lighting the way. There wasn't anything except a soft radio playing in the background.

"Hello Julia, I have been expecting you. Oh don't take the stairs; you know how cranky the Nagas can get." His voice called to me through the vast darkness and dim soft lighting.

"Good evening Morning Star, yes I remember." I said and smiled as I hung my overcoat on the hooks along the wall.

I instantly let my wings rip out of my back and clothes. I flew to him carrying a box with a red bow on top. I know what you are thinking; a human with wings is pretty far-fetched right? But what you don't know is that I had evolved a long time ago. I was able to hide through sorcery. It was a simple glamour spell that he had taught me, nothing much really. But I never had to hide when I was with him. I was normal when I was with him. I felt like he had saved me so many times. He really was my angel.

The caves candles seemed to grow brighter and then I heard him snap his fingers and many dazzling crystal chandeliers turned on. There were many tiny little crystals adorning the cave walls adding to a refracted rainbow effect; and glittering light off the black stone they were poking out of.

The throne room was so incredibly large. I'm positive millions of souls could fit in here. But the truth was they were all part of the reset. I wondered where our energy would travel once we were all destroyed. I quickly focused on the box I was carrying and brought it to him as he sat in his grand throne at a large golden table.

Immediately his doe like ears perked up and his big red eyes grew large. His smile was large and endearing, even as his fangs seemed to grow in delight.

"Oh you remembered. Thank you Julia I think I will miss this the most." His deep voice echoed his happiness off the cave walls.

"I couldn't let you leave without one more treat for the road." I said as I tried to hold my smile.

He delicately took off the ribbon and then took a giant lemon cream-filled donut out of the bakery box using his large black clawed fingers.

"You know Julia this is my favorite in the entire world. That bakery is simple divine. Thank you so much my friend." His deep raspy voice was strong and gracious even with his magnificent jewel encrusted, golden crown sitting on his head.

I was in awe of my company even though we had been best friends for the last seven years. He was just too glorious for words.

"I will definitely miss that bakery. Hopefully in the next round we find it again. Are the others on their way?" I said as I couldn't help but be lost in his eyes every time he looked at me.

"We have some company coming. They should be here at the stroke of ten." His deep loving voice captivated me.

"Darn, I was hoping to get you all to myself." I said and winked while smiling mischievously.

"You make me blush Julia. Besides I have more contracts than yours. You are just one of the noblest souls I don't have to hunt down later." He said and I knew I was making him blush, but I couldn't stop being enchanted by him.

"I know what I did. But I also know what you have given me. Time will fly faster than we both know. Speaking of which, how much time is God giving you?" I said but now my eyes lingered on his full lips and then bounced to his strong red jawline.

"Well, I shall have to be fully transformed and ready to go by three.

Those sealed doors will open. The fallen angels will then rise and be set free from this prison. We are given the task of hunting down the wicked and slaughtering them brutally. And that will be a task in itself; all while the 6th horn of the rapture is sounding off annoyingly throughout the lands. Only three hours are we given to harvest souls. The fallen angels are the Nagas as you know. They are resting until they transform or they eat; or whichever comes first. It is a good thing we have had centuries to focus on the scent." His strong voice seemed to be mesmerizing as I tried to focus on his eyes instead of his lips and brooding muscular chest.

"Tell me what does the wicked smell like Morning Star?" I said as I sat beside him at the table and he snapped his fingers and a coffee appeared in front of me.

"Well only in the last three hours before the end of the world; I asked the Father if I could make the evil souls smell so strongly like these cream-filled donuts so we the fallen could sniff them out easier; and he said; *"Yes"*. This scent will make us so ravenous no one will be able to hide as we devour meat and suck up souls." He said with so much glee he had this beautiful twinkle in his eyes and a cool chill ran down my back.

I smiled at him warmly and nodded as he passed me honey and cream for my coffee. I knew it was his duty. My death, as was everyone in the entire planet, was absolute. But yet I felt opposite to humanity. I felt like I had never fit in. He was the only one who had made me feel like I belonged. And I did. I belonged to him. I held my cup of warmth and embraced my future of mere hours now. Literally there was no where I wanted to be other than right here with him.

My heart raced at being alone with him right now; even though we had always been alone together in the last seven years. But this time, I started remembering our love making from past lives and suddenly felt hot with desire. It didn't even matter I was on the menu tonight.

CHAPTER 3

ONLY HUMAN

I couldn't describe the feeling I got whenever I was with him. Here he was, this supernatural being sitting before me. With everything I had seen in my life, he had been the best part. He was far from the bad guy the world had led the masses to believe.

Human minds with free will were far more evil than anything he had tried to plague humanity with. We were our own undoing. I think everyone deep down knew this globally as soon as they started developing nuclear weapons to defeat the doomsday asteroid, seven years ago. We were our own bringers of destruction and what had killed the planet before the asteroid had even entered our orbit.

As humans we had it backwards to some degree. The Morning Star was created with purpose from the All High. He was created by the Divine to lead the stray, and then capture the lost wicked souls. It wasn't his fault he excelled at his job and that we were so obliging.

We definitely had it wrong. We had become the monsters that monsters fear. We were too blind to see the future when it was still in our hands.

"Julia you're making me blush." His deep voice sounded silvery smooth now and I realized I had been staring into his eyes lost in thought.

"Sorry I was just thinking about humanity's not so great ideas; like using the Ark of the Covenant. Who could have seen how bad that idea was? Like we could ever use that power and yield it to destroy the asteroid." I said and shrugged as I watched his cheeks turn an even rosier shade when I smiled.

"It's okay you know. You can ask me anything before the others get here. Isn't there some great secret of the universe that you might want to know?" He said warmly as his deep voice seemed to soothe my soul every time I heard it.

He seemed to float to the oven and it hadn't even occurred to me that he would be making his guests treats until the aroma coming from the open oven door hit my nostrils. *Mmm...chocolate chip cookies.* He could have used magic but I assumed he was saving his strength for the final curtain call of the world.

I enjoyed the personal touches of him actually baking the cookies. I also enjoyed the fact he never needed oven mitts. It really was these little gestures that always made me smile. Pulling burning things out of the oven was grand in itself, but boy did he make the most delicious cookies on the whole face of this earth. He had created spices that were out-of-this realm fantastic.

"Can I offer you some cookies?" He said and smiled sweetly as his doe-like ears perked up again and his eyes twinkled like a galaxy of stars.

"You know I can never resist you." I said and then blushed as I turned away from his dazzling eyes.

THE HOUSE WINS: APOCALYPTIC FRIENDS TO LOVERS

I took one and it burnt my fingers, but this pain felt good. It felt good to be living, even if it was only for another five and half more hours. It was a little hard to grasp when you knew in less than six hours I would cease to exist. Actually, we would all cease to exist.

After the fallen angels ravaged and scavenged the world collecting sinful, unrepentant souls then the Great War would begin. But the deck was stacked and even my best friend knew this; they all did. The house wins always. Good would win this round and then everything would reset and it would all begin again.

The darkness had the same fate. But at least they had front row seats. My seat had been like that of someone not even in the stadium. I wouldn't even get to watch the game. My soul would go to the abyss, and if I was fortunate I would have another inning to play again when the game reset. Luck was always in the eye of the beholder though. Because after the great reset, life would be even harder just like every time had been.

Almost every life of mine had ended in his loving arms. I was quite lucky. There were a few cowardly lives where he had to hunt me down; but in my opinion those other past me's had deserved it. He was a noble being. A bringer of truth and if you made the deal you had to pay. It made me feel ashamed to think of those lives I had been living; when I had lived in Atlantis. I shuddered as I remembered his anger and the pained expression he had made right before he got me.

"Such past events should stay there Julia. It is no good to dwell on such things especially when you are here with me now. Be present for the time moves quickly and the veil grows thinner as we sit and enjoy coffee and cookies before the others get here." His voice was deep and sizzling.

"You are right. Thank you for making your special cookies. It really isn't the end of the world without them. Sometimes I get flooded all at once of memories of all the past lives and it gets to me." I said and ate another offered cookie.

As our hands touched more memories of us in the past being intimate emerged and I tried not to dwell on those happy fantasies. Angels didn't need the same kind of intimacy as humans desired. But here the memories flashed through my mind and I couldn't help but close my eyes while I felt my pulse quicken and my cheeks getting hotter by the second.

"Maybe I should crack a window my little human or you shall enthrall all of hell in our awakening of each other's bodies again." He said whimsically and I felt awkward of my dirty thoughts that he was keenly aware of.

I closed my eyes and focused on how delicious the cookies were but my animalistic thoughts quickly returned to how wonderful his lips tasted and his blood. I could feel my fangs slightly elongating as the memories of us drinking each other's blood stirred my soul deeply.

When I opened my eyes I watched him trying to find something out of a massive cupboard. I walked over to him and put my arms around his backside.

"Let me help you. I bet I know which platter you are looking for and I bet I can get to it faster than you can." I said sweetly and winked.

"Really, would you like to wager?"

"Yes I would." I said and grinned.

"Name your price Julia. Anything can be yours when it's the end of the world." He said with a smile as I was already slipping in front of him to take on the battle of the cluttered cupboard.

"If I find it, I want you to kiss me like the world is on fire and we are the last beings in creation. And I also want you to tell me something I don't know about you." I said and climbed into the darkness after quickly grabbing his hand to shake on it.

"Fine it is done. But if I win you must do what I say and not question me or my motives." His deep voice soothed my soul even though I was curious.

"Well of course, I won't question you, but what is it you wish me to do?" I said casually as I kept searching.

"I cannot tell you right now. But I will tell you closer to the time when it will be imperative for you to listen to me." His voice seemed to lack the strength and it seemed strained.

I took one look at him and nodded cheerfully, okay.

Then we suddenly shouted; "Found it" at the same time.

"So I guess it is a tie. Do we both get what we want then?" I said and smirked as I passed him the golden lid of the Ark of the Covenant.

"Yes, I guess we both can win this time." He said smiling as he took the lid and my fingers softly grazed his electric skin.

We started piling cookies and desserts on the lid. The entire time I was teasing him about using the lid as a platter.

"Waste not want not. This one was used anyways and it had been in a storage hanger for years. So I acquired it for my home away from home." His said and his fanged smile was contagious.

"Well naturally, the Ark of the Covenant is of course the ultimate in high fashion and décor. Just think of all the décor trends you'll be starting once this gets out. All the ladies will love you and your desserts now." I said and teasingly slapped his bottom with the tea towel.

"I only have eyes for one lady, thank you very much…Hey…Not fair my hands are full." He shouted with glee as he carried the platter to a smaller table along the cave wall while I continued to get in a few more cheap shots.

When he turned around he snapped his fingers and he now had a tea towel too. I squealed with laughter as he tried to get me back and missed. We had wild smiles as we chased each other around the table.

Then I accidently slipped and we fell together to the floor. As I laughed with him, I couldn't help but be so enraptured in his closeness.

My breathing was just as heavy as his and it felt like our chests were rising and falling in intervals that mirrored each other but fit. He felt so warm underneath me and I just wanted to lose myself in his arms as he held me. His perfect fanged smile was right there and I could see the way his eyes were drawn to my forbidden lips as I lingered in his strong arms.

"We...we should get ready they will be here soon." He said and I agreed slowly getting up; trying hard to hide my disappointment.

I nodded that he was right and reached out my hand to help him up. He happily took my hand and got back on both hooves. But as he stood there he continued to still hold my hand. His hand was gently caressing mine as he looked down into my eyes.

"You know Julia you have retained memories that I have not had the luxury of knowing yet. I am always left in the dark as my memories get wiped with every reset. But when I look at you I feel there has always been something more. It is something just out of my grasp. It is like knowing you belong in the world because someone special makes your life better in every way. My darkness seems to have golden sunshine raining through my clouds because of you. I feel strange and not myself when you are around. As you know, I have duties to perform which are not so pleasant but you make me feel that I could drop everything and run away with you. You make me feel like eternity could be filled with something so forbidden and sweet that I could only dream about." His voice was so gentle as he rested his lips on my forehead breathing me in deeply, and then he cleared his throat breaking some moonlight spell.

"But you need to know; and your soul needs to remember this time. Angels and humans were never allowed to love each other as intimate as your eyes long for mine. I can sense the shadow of light across my heart. It is forbidden in all the realms and in all the galaxies Julia. So it would be better if we just forgot any past life relations. All I can offer you is my personal neverending friendship. It is yours for all of eternity; just for you Julia." He whispered breathless into my hair as the radio played a soft medley and he started slowly dancing with me.

"I remember being struck by lightning from the heavens the first time we kissed. I know it is forbidden and I know you are right. But I can still dream with you can't I?" I said while closing my eyes and resting my head against his fierce beating heart.

We slowly swayed together as the soft music continued to play in the background somewhere deep in the unforgiving darkness. As I closed my eyes my hand gently caressed his horns and then his face. For the first time I heard him sigh so heavenly, as I continued to caress his face and then traced his skin down his neck and across his strong shoulders. His lips lightly brushed my hair and then down my forehead across my nose and cheek. His breathing was heavier as was mine as he held me tighter and danced even slower holding me tighter; while it felt like time stopped.

🌾🌾🌾🌾

CHAPTER 4

DESSERT LID OF GREATNESS

This cave of magic and mystery; this was the doorway to hell and yet here is where my soul always longed for. This space in-between good and evil; right and wrong; this was the place I always wanted to be. And it was always with him. This forbidden yearning wasn't rational though and I tried to focus on setting the table with poker chips as he had stopped dancing to take some more cookies out of the oven.

My soul was remembering even more of this night and this poker game. The past events which always seemed to play out exactly the same for each life time fascinated me. It was as if my soul was tied to a neverending situation and final outcome which played consistently on a loop.

I was looking forward to the guests that always came here with my soul. There was a very holy werewolf named Jack; one Leprechaun named Thomas; and a dark unicorn named Ralph. Soon they would stroll in and the game would begin. The prize was always the same. The winner would get to be the last one sacrificed to the darkness. But we all longed for this; more so than not.

I started stacking the insignificant chips while my lovely host started placing even more cookies on the golden lid which dazzled with the stardust from the Ether. Even this half of the coveted treasure that mankind had fought many wars over was displayed beautifully. The wings had held cookies in every crevice. The more I smelt the delicious aromas the more my smile beamed. For the end of the world this really was the place to be.

I glanced over to my friend and caught him observing me and then he quickly turned away to add rose petals as decorations. Although I could not see the redness of his cheeks while his face was turned from me; I smiled because I knew it was there. He was such a bashful, graceful creature of habit. I wished his memories of us together in past lives would return before the others got here.

I focused back on the dessert platter of greatness. Such a thing that oozed power and riches; and now it was reduced to a dessert serving platter. Humans had fought humans for the power the other half of this box structure had held for millennia. I listened past the radio sounds hearing the screams and explosions of the chaos outside. It astounded me the scale of the true war of the light against the darkness. In the smallest of terms we had been stupid in accidently destroying the earth instead of the asteroid with all the Arks. Then the Angels stepped in. *What a relief that was.* I had lingered in that thought and stood staring at my friends red glowing eyes; so beautiful and so mysterious.

He flashed his razor smile and I sighed in my ongoing fantasy love of him. He oozed this sexual magnetic charm even the holiest of nuns could not resist. He could kill them with just one alluring look from those sexy eyes. I envied him.

"Sorry I was just thinking about the wars over the 13 Arks of the Covenant." I said and quickly looked over to the world clock that seemed to be even gloomier with this dark mist hanging around it.

"I know what you have been thinking. But you need not worry about the Arks; nor the meteor that comes to destroy us; or the end of life as we know it my little Flame." His deep voice soothed and seduced my souls' senses.

I felt like moving closer to him now to take him in my arms and never let him go but I remained seated and glued beside the table. I heard louder noises suddenly breaking my trance of doom and gloom and more unrequited love.

The noises were getting unbearably louder and louder. He instinctively stood up and moved towards the stairs but stopped where I stood. He placed his large hand on my shoulder and I grabbed it. I needed his comfort just now. I placed my hand on his and gave his skin a quick kiss; closing my eyes tight. I always longed for more time with him. It was never enough and the end of the world always came without mercy and quicker each time. Each life it was the same. He would always realize my undying love just as the others arrived. Each time it was the same, we would end up missing the opportunity of hours we could have been in each other's arms. It was always too late and had always been to forbidden to even think of; yet I always did.

"I know now Julia. Your memories of thoughts have just flashed before my eyes of your unbridled passion. I have felt your yearning as if it was my own and I am now hungered for your love. The blood you give in each lifetime lets me feel the unconditional love you have for me in your heart. That is the real reason you are here with me now. That is why you have chosen to be here in most every life time. I remember now. But there is never the time of love between angels and humans; even in the end as the world clock ticks to the beat of our doomed hearts.

THE HOUSE WINS: APOCALYPTIC FRIENDS TO LOVERS

Your love will reunite in energy across the universe to mine. And I will be there in the darkness always waiting to hold you my Love. No matter the outcome; I will find you no matter what." He said and I knew he spoke the truth but I couldn't stop the tears.

I knew the end was never the end. It was just each time it felt like it took longer and longer for our love to find each other; in all the different past lives. I squeezed his hand and kissed it again as I heard grumpy voices and hisses. The guests were always clumsy and loud; awakening the Nagas. I stole one more kiss against his strong red skin and then placed my hand on my mug of coffee.

I was looking down when he suddenly took my hand from my mug and brought me gently to my feet. I was now being carried in his arms as he wrapped me in the warmth of his soft black feathered wings which only a moment before had resembled leather.

The ticking of the clock had stopped as he held me. The noises had stopped and everything had become deadly quiet. It was only us and it felt like he was giving me an eternity's worth of embraces in this moment of stolen frozen time.

"Julia you are what I shall miss more than I can express in words. All of our time together through all of the wars and resets; have made me just now realize I love you. For you I am stopping time just to steal you away and hold you. I need to touch your skin to mine. I need all of you; so dark and forbidden. And I need you now before our world ends. I need you before I change back to my original beauty. I need to feel you loving me with all my grotesqueness." He said as he cupped my cheek and I gazed into his enchanting red glowing eyes.

"You have never been grotesque to me my lovely Morning Star. The ideologies and cruelness that the world has made of you is grotesque. You are so beautiful and magmatic my Prince; my Love. I would die happily in your arms and have my last breath in an eternal kiss with just the touch of your lips; than spend another second without your love." I said as he kissed me and carried me to his private quarters.

I could feel his heart thundering against my chest. Both of us knew this was forbidden as our layers peeled off faster than I could say the words abracadabra. Angels didn't need the same kind of affections that humans did; but he did from me. We both hungered for each other's touch as soon as the memories of love first aroused our spirits. Our hands caressed each other so lovingly as we kissed and indulged in the sweetness of love. I had erupted in an uncontained enrapture of need greater than my soul could hold back and matched his unabashed pleasure fest. After each climax he sank his fangs over my heart to drink of my love and after he gasped I sank my fangs into his chest drinking just as heavy the loving life force beating together in our veins. Our love was a loving sticky, mess of us as we rolled around in the red satin sheets. Our love was a palpitating, throbbing fanatical adoration that exploded in the most freakishly loving rhapsody of excited sweat; loving blood; and joyous tears.

After, we lay there trying to catch our breath but continuing to indulge in sweet kisses and real-life fantasies of each other. I clung to his naked body and lay my face across his chest as he slowly traced my arm back and forth with his fingers while still embracing me. *This is my heaven.* Here we stayed in each other's arms with even softer kisses and softer whispers of love. Even in his force of need, he was gentle with me using his heavenly powers. There was nothing in the galaxy of stars or the universe that compared to the sweetness of his soul to mine.

"This moment I shall cherish with you forever Julia." He cooed in my ear as he kissed me and squeezed me in his arms.

"I have loved you always and you are my forever. I needed this moment alone with you...I needed you before..."

"Sssssh, I know Julia. I needed your love and your touch just as much. I needed our skin to melt together like one. I needed to be even closer to you." He whispered as he gave me another tight squeeze.

I treasured being embraced in his love and his safe strong arms. I adored the way he tasted my loving soul's blood. I could feel him draining my soul in pure ecstasy and it felt miraculous to give him what my words could not express. Only my heart space could give him what he needed to know. When he let me taste his loving essence of blood; it was the most incredible surge of magic and eternal love all throughout my entire body. His abundant life force made me quake and shiver from his absolute passionate hunger of my soul. I could feel his monstrous affection, throbbing into my open being even as I lay there and he moved slowly while my body shook from intense desire.

What humans had forgotten was that angels had been made first. They were all beings of love. All angels were tapped in directly to the source of creation and he was no exception. When he erupted I felt his ultimate power of unconditional supernatural love and it moved me to tears as he collapsed on me now so vulnerable.

I think maybe this was why my DNA had changed as we lay there trying to catch our breath between erotic kisses. But that thought and the world ending left as quickly as it had come. In this moment there was only us. I secretly wished we could stay here in this existence of a mere moment of frozen time together for all of eternity.

"If I was allowed to wish I would stay here with you throughout existence my love. But let us get ready my little Flame. Be strong. I promise there is no realm in which can stop our love in finding a way back to each other. We have been married in the underworld of the heavens and I can never be without you my bride." His voice was deep but loving as he started kissing me again.

I nodded and kissed him back as true as my heart could reveal. I wiped my eyes after he had not been able to stop the little droplets from coming. I nodded again and stuck my chin out. I needed to be brave now. I needed to be brave for him. He snapped his fingers; and now he was wearing a blue pin-striped suit and I was wearing a matching indigo over-one-shoulder Grecian toga. My wrists were adorned with golden bracelets and my ring finger held a red sun-sapphire golden ring. He had healed most fang marks across my body except the two punctured marks over my heart and I smiled as I felt the loving scars that appeared.

He carried me back to my seat beside his glorious golden throne at the large table. He kissed me long and slow, suddenly sitting me on the table and hiking up my long dress. He opened my legs firmly as he kissed me harder and I started to undue his belt and pants. His emotions were overflowing filling both our need to fulfill his monstrous throbbing and enraptured heated passion. As we squeezed and moved in another round of forbidden relishing of our entangled bodies; tenderly he bit my breast and once more drank my loving energy as he now transformed to his full angel gloriousness. He took me to his throne as we moved even faster and he offered his neck to me. Grateful for his kindness I drank hearty of his loving blood before we climaxed in harmonious screams of pleasure. Then he kissed me deeply before whispering in an angelic language he loved me.

"I love you too and I will love you forever my beautiful Morning Star." I whispered as he kissed me embracing my tight.

"Kittens. One thing you don't know about me is I like kittens. But don't tell anyone." He whispered as he kissed me again sweeping me up into his arms.

While lovingly kissing me he took me back to his private little waterfall in his shower room. We intimately showered together to get ready again for the guests; stealing more heart racing moments.

Then once again he snapped his fingers and we were back seated at the table. He was back in another pin-striped-suit (The first one had been ripped apart), while he sat on his golden throne. I was back seated beside him in a matching azure Grecian over-one-shoulder toga. I was still adorned with large golden bracelets as gifts he had given me. His sweet kisses had sealed over the punctured fang marks in a loving scar once more. My large golden wedding ring seemed to be glowing from our love as was my heart.

Then my handsome Morning Star kissed me once more leaving me swooning with his angel stardust in my eyes. If I had been standing I would have fainted right there as he smiled to me with rosy cheeks.

Just then he gave me a more serious look though and I nodded bravely with my brightest and biggest smile. It was time.

Without any more pausing or notice; he snapped his fingers and the giant world clock started ticking again and the lights became brighter as the world around us resumed. The guests became more boisterous as they neared the top of the stairs.

I smiled warmly as I wiped one last escaped tear and straightened my back to become more presentable. *I will miss you my best friend.*

🌿🌿🌿

CHAPTER 5

THE GUESTS

Time had liberated as the guests came thumping up the stairs completely oblivious to the stolen hours. It made me happy to know that our forbidden love was stronger than their contracts. I felt relieved in having more time with him before the end of the world.

Everyone was taking their seats and I froze as I noticed two new faces. Through all the knowledge of my past lifetimes; these two individuals had never had seats at the table. It disturbed me that this lifetime was very different and these new guests were proof. New beings were not allowed at this table not on this day. It was an honor to be here.

You didn't have to be ultra-evil for the grand doors of the temple to open and for a seat here with us. In fact a lot of us dark creatures weren't here for what we did, although we had done something to get notice by the all-spark.

We were all here because we were noble to a point. No one had helped us or persuaded us into joining the dark side. We were here as willing sacrifices bound in a blood pact; and the two new creatures were not. I could smell something else off them as I knew the others had.

Jack had his nostrils flaring but did not say a word except greeted me and then gave me a certain knowing look. Whatever these two new beings were playing at; it was not for us to intercede. The Morning Star knew thoughts and deeds; and I would not dare to mess with such a heavenly being tasked with such greatness as soul harvesting. These two new creatures I loathed instantly and remembered that they usually loitered outside of the temple's heavy cast iron doors. They were the disgusting creatures usually first to be slaughtered and then harvested.

It took me only one moment to recognize the vampire Avaricio and a dark elf named Luxuria. Both had very long blonde hair; pointed ears and blood stained fangs. And both were stunning. I couldn't tell if it was magic or if Avaricio really was that glamourous; as he introduced himself and started eating before our kind host had even offered.

Luxuria had sparkling green eyes and her skin was a pale shade of lavender. She was sinfully erotic. She was scantily clad and with reason. She had been bragging about how easy it was to seduce mortal men and then rob them with the dagger she had stashed in her boot. She was also bragging about how she could tempt anyone, just long enough before finishing them. Her breasts were large and obnoxious just like her ego.

I rolled my eyes as she faked a polite giggle when a chair was pulled out for her and her breasts jiggled as she laughed. Her leather halter top barely had enough fabric to cover her satin flesh as did her leather loin cloth. I thought about ordering her a towel to sit on, so her unique outfit wouldn't leave a mark on the seats if she was too excited, but then changed my mind from speaking. Just then I caught Morning Star looking at me so mischievous and a smirk came across his face. *Darn you heard my thought. I'm sorry but she is dressed to kill, isn't she? Why is she here now?* My thoughts had been making my friend smile so beautifully I blushed at his radiance.

"Hello Julia, it is Julia right?" her silver voice oozed seduction and my pulse quickened which shocked me.

"Hello Luxuria, I may be only human but isn't it a little cold for that outfit? I mean with all the missiles that have been going off it definitely has gotten colder outside. Are you dressed warm enough for the apocalypse?" I asked although her halter top was more like a leather ribbon precariously across her heavy chest and opened quite frequently.

"It has gotten a little chilly but I am too excited to notice. But I'm sure you can see that for yourself. It has been raining fire balls all day long and I have been driving mortal men absolutely mad with all the desire I have been radiating. I can tell you this; it wouldn't matter what I was wearing. I can seduce anyone at any time." Luxuria had this raspy voice deceptively rich with sweetness and I almost believed she cared for one second.

But I knew better.

I watched her give a sinful wink to my best friend; and then she plumped her lips to make a kiss me face as she mal-adjusted her shirt on purpose to him. Instantly, I could feel my cheeks heat with a secret rage.

To my admiration, my best friend met her eyes with an icy-eyed glance. Now his red skin was gone and his true golden skin was radiating as he had transformed completely to his original heavenly form. He snapped his fingers and Luxuria was dressed completely in a red hooded sweatshirt and red oversized sweat pants.

Luxuria instantly frowned as she realized what had happened and gave me a scornful look while I just smiled. Her displeasure gave me great satisfaction and I didn't hide it. Why should I? It was the end of the world and I didn't need her eye candy around my angel. This is when I grinned and let my fangs elongate in front of her. I contemplated something dark; knowing I could do something right now to her with no regrets, but quickly decided against ruining the party.

Jack had looked at me with raised eyebrows and then suddenly howled in agony. He transformed beside me quite suddenly. He was unable to stop and in horrible pain. I couldn't help myself from saying a silent prayer for my werewolf friend. I hated seeing Jack suffer. It wasn't his fault he was born into the darkness; yet he was the most pure soul I had ever met. He was no less evil than the ancient little leprechaun across the table from me.

When Jack's spine cracked back into place and his bones shrank back to normal; his torn fur revealed his pale skin underneath. I crouched down and hugged his bare bloody back.

"Oh Jack." I said as he turned and hugged me back.

"I'm ok. I'm just looking forward to this rest. I am so tired of being hunted and this time the change has been almost unbearable." Jack whispered and thanked me for moving in front of him to cover him with my dress.

I looked over to my beautiful best friend's blue eyes that looked like steel but he snapped his fingers and instantly Jack was dressed in a white hoodie and jogging pant suit.

"Thank you my Morning Star. I hope I didn't ruin the party." Jack said out of breath as the sweat dripped down his forehead still.

"You have never ruined anything Jack ever." My best friend said and I smiled and mouthed the words *thank you* as I helped Jack to his chair beside me.

My beautiful angel winked and smiled sweetly at me; and I swiftly took my seat back beside him. But Jack needed a moment to regain his composure. I let him rest his head on my shoulder while I rubbed his arm and tried to soothe him. His breath was harder than all those times in the woods when I had found him and he needed me more than ever before as his heavy arm went around me. His eyes were closed as he regained his strength and I noticed this strange, small white star shape in his black hair.

Meanwhile Ralph was belching loudly. He was completely ignoring everyone as he pounded back pink beer from somewhere over the rainbow I suppose. Ralph was a unicorn. But he wasn't like the other loving, magical beasts. He was far from the creations of light actually. He was loud, rude and falling apart quite literally at the table. The only thing about him that was different was a similar white star on his dark matted chest. It stood out like sunshine against his coarse black fur.

Luxuria was smiling wickedly at Jack and I was grateful Jack's eyes were still closed.

"Why do I taste corn? For crying out loud Ralph; not at the table." Jack snapped and then suddenly sat up.

Jack waved his hand in the air around his nose and I almost gaged at the foul odor in the air. Jack looked dashing even scrunching up his nose in Ralph's smiling direction. Something seemed to change in Jack since the last time I had seen him one week ago. He was much more ruggedly handsome. I watched Luxuria studying him as if she had read my mind. Even with his sneered expression; Jack could be a cover model. Ralph started laughing and farted again; breaking up my thoughts which I was thankful for.

"Ralph I will have to plug a certain orifice of yours, if you choose to continue. But it is your freewill to do whatever it is you please." His voice seemed light-hearted but we all looked at Ralph and knew he was pushing his luck with our gracious host.

"I can stop passing gas from my glorious derriere anytime but I cannot stop belching occasionally from all the magical barley I have consumed. This pink ale is not only self-gratifying but also medicinal and necessary as you can all see by now." When Ralph spoke so eloquently my jaw dropped.

His façade was the best in centuries. I don't think I'd ever met such a deceptively clever individual in my whole existence pardoned to one. I had forgotten that Ralph was centuries old. Most unicorns were good and holy but not Ralph. He was a pure night-breed created to bring chaos into all mortal's (not just humans) dreams.

The more I looked at Ralph's glare the more I seen his eyes strain to retain this dignity of filthy-rage. He was slowly seeping out this black, sparkly, tarred-ooze from his ears; and his eyes had this blue-glaze over them from the onset blindness creeping in. It was clear Ralph was dying right there at the table. The drinks he had been downing truly were medicinal and I wondered what had happened to him this time. He was always picking absurd fights in an attempt to bring disharmony to everyone.

Foolishly, I knocked my napkin to the floor and when I picked it up I glanced across the table to see Ralph's hooves oozing as well as a large gash across his legs. I paused to see Avaricio collecting large amounts of Ralph's blood in his goblet and gasped as he smiled wickedly at me.

When I returned upright in my chair I noticed Ralph's directed gazed wrath at me. His blue-black eyes were just like his heart and soul; void of all goodness. But that patch of white on Ralph's fur seemed to shine. I gasped again as Ralph scooped his own blood from his oozing ear and tried to rub the glow from his chest out. He sneered at me with gritted teeth before Jack elbowed me to stop looking. Then Jack gave me a look and I nodded right before he squeezed my arm gently.

Jack was my other best friend. We always found each other in each lifetime, in different wildernesses of the world. We always met young; and in hiding from the government. It's fair to say I loved Jack with every bit of my being. I was his guardian and he was mine. Our soul's journey together never stopped in all lifetimes, and in all underworlds.

Jack was actually a good guy. It really wasn't his fault his bloodline had been cursed. His soul was clean and pure. He only fed off deer and rabbits when he was transformed. A flashback suddenly came to me of Jack in his human form trying to keep warm through winter and I blushed at those loving memories. Then, I heard a loud throat clear and stopped focusing my thoughts on such innocent love. I turned my attention to all of the guests; the food; and the game of all games.

This was a special game of sorts for the outcasts of society. I fit along here with Jack. We both had never felt real companionship or real friendship with anyone other than the Morning Star; and he had graciously opened his arms completely for all of us.

We were all oddities in the universe. The anomalies of living creatures that were considered to many as *'textbook evil'*; but the truth of our souls had proven that we all weren't or just couldn't be. There was another realm of darkness in the Ether for all of us; apart from the fire pits that awaited most damned souls. And I remembered always being there with Jack.

The realm I ended up with Jack was an in-between realm. Other humans had referred to it as a purgatory of darkness. I was always there with Jack and the other werewolves in our pack. It was a realm of only darkness but we were happy. We lived for this realm and the great servitude. We were the guardians of the lost children. It was in this realm that I had my very first encounter of Jack. He was pushing a lost child on a swing. This realm was the in-between before the light came for the child's soul to be reincarnated. Our duty was actually a peaceful job. We were the protectors; it was kind of an unpaid civil service job. But I loved being there with him.

The realm was created for those innocent souls who didn't know they were dead. Angels were always coming and going from this place. The angels would take the precious souls onward and upward to this other realm of radiant light and warmth. I turned my thoughts back to the coffee and cookies I was being offered.

Then I looked over to Jack and felt like I just saw him for the first time. His features were striking and he was quite large and muscular in human form. I felt him place his arm around me and we both drank more coffee in unison. He was my pack and I was his always; even though I had never been reincarnated as a werewolf on earth.

Everyone at the table was chit chatting as I just enjoyed this rich coffee with Jack. Jack had gone to clutching his mug so tightly for warmth that I placed my arm around him and gave him a squeeze. He tapped my mug in cheers and then we drank. Our cups were never emptying; the magic in the cave knew your souls desires. Jack's thoughts were commenting to me about how much he would miss coffee and I answered in agreement through my mind to him. Coffee was a luxury we wouldn't be having in any scenario of realms we had ever ended up in. They didn't have coffee in the underworld; although you could drink it from the entire pool of lawyer's blood. We had always opted out of that option. The truth was that souls rarely changed even after death. It was not unheard of though. The Holy Spirit surprised us all the time in transforming someone to the light. I smiled at our thoughts but stopped our mental communication as I saw a slight red flash behind my glorious best friend's blue eyes.

"Please everyone enjoy the food and drink. There is still time before we begin." Our gorgeous host said as his deep voice triggered a slight longing I tried to subdue again.

I sat there and watched the well-dressed vampire known as Avaricio just now as he had caught my eye. You might know dear reader Avaricio by another name. And his name suits him from what I was compelled to keep watching.

Avaricio was bottling up Ralph's tar-filled blood and filling his pockets with the tiny jars. Not only that, he was drinking the blood in his goblet. He was adding the secret ingredient to each of his three drinks. Avaricio had a beer, a coffee and a goblet (which only contained a little of the wine he had started with). He was drinking these three drinks because he could never have the will to choose only one. I think if I was closer he would have tried to drink my coffee along with his. But seeing him scooping more blood was purely disgusting and I tried not to turn up my nose at his hunger. But my distaste for Avaricio using poor Ralph was undeniable.

But Ralph was enjoying himself a little too much. He couldn't care what anyone else was doing here. He was only here for one purpose and all of us knew it. And it was about getting shit faced even though we knew he already was.

🌾🌾🌾🌾

CHAPTER 6

THE GAME

Ralph always lost at poker. For all the lifetimes I could remember; he had only one purpose to be here at the end of the world. He was meat. He was meat for the beasts. We all were in some way or another. The fallen needed food before bringing wrath to the chaotic world. Ralph prided himself on being sacrificed as a grand meal for the darkness.

I wasn't sure if he lost on purpose. Who knows really? All I knew was that this time was different from all the other lifetimes of games that I could recall. Ralph had never had a white spot of light on him. Come to think of it neither did Jack. I gasped in silent horror as I looked down and saw the same white star shape on my tanned hand as the cards were being dealt.

Everyone in mere seconds had stopped eating and drinking and was now looking at each of their five cards. I quickly picked mine up and studied them. Then I rolled my eyes and tried not to laugh. Maybe this game wasn't as different as all the others after all.

Everyone seemed to be contemplating too hard except Ralph. He threw all his chips into the center and loudly declared; "All in."

"Ralph it is only eleven thirty three, you know the rules. You cannot go all in until the third hand. Please stick to honoring my company and the game." His deep voice gently warned.

"Yes, my liege but you have already transformed as did the magic in this temple. I have seen the dark feathers floating in the breezeless air." Ralph said as he belched loudly and blew it in all of our groaning directions making it smell like a raw sewage treatment plant.

"Come on Ralph. Even if I was hungry I'm not now." Jack said and laughed.

We were all part of the same magic of creation and it would be like cannibalism to him and me. Of course the others weren't bothered as I gazed at their hungry eyes and salivating fangs towards Ralph.

I just looked over to my best friend who was looking at me and then quickly turned to his cards uninterested in everything except the game. He studied his hand and then flashed his warm gaze back at me and I blushed. He really had noticeably changed to his even more beautiful angel form. His hair was a golden shoulder length blonde. His eyes were this striking pale blue and his skin seemed to shimmer with this eternal sun-kissed quality. He was more magnificent than human words could describe. He seemed to glitter with every slight movement he made. I sighed at seeing his splendor and how much I wanted to kiss his red plump lips but couldn't. Instead I turned to my hand and tried to remember the rules.

The rules were pretty clear though:

1. Three hands were a must. You had to stay in the game for a minimum of the first three hands.

2. It was a five card draw or whatever was dealt to you at the time.

3. "All In" wasn't an option until after the third game. Then if you wanted to fulfill your greatest destiny you could step up to the plate by all means necessary.

4. Only after the third hand was your soul released from this table. Until then all our souls were tied to this moment of required socialness. No matter what happened to the rest of the world even if the temple cave fell apart.

5. The Grand Host is the soul judge and any misdemeanors found in contempt of the game rules of social etiquette will result in disqualification and an early termination of contract.

I remember several lifetimes of the cave walls being blasted through and watching the screaming chaotic mess outside. There really were horrors going on outside the walls surrounding our safe haven. We were helpless to move and helpless to save anyone if we chose. Jack always tried to attempt to help; but even as he stood up, he was ordered to sit back down and he obeyed. No one could betray the prime directive of our social requirements to the game. Even our dialogue was scripted from all the lifetimes before in a never ending loop.

But this game was slightly different I could feel the magic surrounding us, just like Ralph had mentioned. Then I gasped as a new player started walking towards the table and another seat magically pulled up in-between Avaricio and Jack. The table enlarged and moved with all us seated; magically there was enough room.

The figure was dressed in an all-black cloak and carried his scythe like a walking cane. His dark black feathers seemed to glitter in the twinkling lights of the crystal embedded walls. I was shocked by his presence and a question flashed through my mind as I seen him approaching.

"The answer to your question is; time waits for no man or beast but it will wait for me Julia. Don't you worry my dear one. I can collect souls and play poker at the same time." The figure spoke as his skeleton hands went up to his dark hood and slowly pulled back the cloak.

I gasped again as he unexpectedly transformed into the archangel he was. His beautiful black wings stretched and then hung close to his back and over his chair. I felt goosebumps from his little flex of his great power that had created a small breeze and his eyes seemed to look deep into my soul. He smiled in an expression of pure genuine warmth and I smiled back harmoniously. He was another being always misunderstood and feared. He was actually a light in the darkness guiding souls on their journey; wherever that might be.

This was another heavenly being that was everywhere all at once and continuously broke the made up rules of time in mankind's society. He was too magical and as magnificent as they come. A normal human would think this archangel's glow was like a permanent ray of sunlight on him. But I knew it was the touch of the divine; it was the touch of God. The Grand Creator was love which manifested as this golden white light of loving energy. All the angels had this same light radiating out of their chest.

I didn't have to ask why he was here. He was here to collect a bunch of us and his presence brought me even more peace. I heard a sigh of relief from Ralph and knew I wasn't alone in my sentiments of Azrael being with us. My soul was just as tired.

Jack suddenly elbowed me and then chuckled as I focused on the game. I had been caught in a daze. I was staring at my best friend and felt one tear come down my cheek. Even though my soul was tired; I loved this mismatched bunch of outcasts.

"Now, now; none of that please Julia." My best friend's deep voice was soothing and I cherished the kindness in his voice.

I nodded as I heard the radio tune to an only-eighties music station in the background. I smiled again regaining my composure. I knocked three times and exchanged three cards for three new cards.

I couldn't resist peeking at Jack's hand as he never held his cards close. Jack was sitting with three aces. Then I looked over to Ralph's wicked smile. Ralph smiled and winked when he showed me his six aces before folding.

My hand held three aces too and I rolled my eyes at the obvious deck flaws that seemed to be always in our favor. The blatant disregarded rules of our supposed five card game of poker; made me roll my eyes again. Jack and I immediately folded at the same time and watched the others playing with determination.

It was going to be a long night I thought as I elbowed Jack gently and he passed me some snacks while he scarfed down a bowl of cheese balls. Then we both enjoyed the salsa and nachos; with Ralph even reaching over the table to indulge. There was a power play between Luxuria and Avaricio at the same time. They were both beat with only having six king's each.

I gasped as I had realized what had just happened though. The giant floating scoreboard marked a giant X by their names. They had lost half of their chips. The first three hands dictated the order of our departures. And now they were both down by one.

Ralph seemed to have black, rolling-smoke coming from his nostrils and his eyes held a red flame I had never witnessed before. We all knew Ralph's strategy and how he longed for the privilege of being eaten first. But this was the first time I heard his hoof stomp and seen the tiny flame coming out of his nostrils.

"Ralph there are still two more hands." I tried to be comforting but it came out more sarcastic and comical as everyone laughed.

Ralph frowned and then nodded solemnly after giving me a death glare. I'm positive he knew what I was thinking and directed his anger my way. But I wasn't concerned with his anger because I knew where it was coming from. I tried to hide the worry in my eyes but my forehead crease always gave me away. This time really was different.

I felt altered. I couldn't explain it. Other than our three new guests; today was changed somehow. I worried about what else was going to change.

Then a small meteor shower took off parts of the wall and a giant hurricane took off the mountain's cave-like roof.

🌾🌾🌾🌾

CHAPTER 7

AVARICIO

Somewhere in-between cards being dealt I had lost track of who had actually won the last hand. All I knew was the earth around us was scorched now and the screaming was being tuned out as the radio suddenly turned up.

We all were dealt a new hand and I was left in a stupor of the chaos unraveling outside. While I looked out the new mountainside windows freshly installed; cars were on fire and buildings in the park had partially collapsed. People were running in the streets with scissors. It was pure chaos. Other forest creatures were coming out of hiding and I wondered if they knew the world was completely ending. They couldn't see us as we all silently watched. Jack and I wore similar horror-filled expressions as we saw a few decapitations.

But Ralph looked furious and his black horn glowed purple and blazed. Avaricio scooped more ooze from Ralph's horn; looking famished and extremely happy at the same time. Luxuria was unconcerned as she gazed at the scythe. It was like the energy at the table had just changed from laughter and playfulness; to anger and necessity.

Ralph hated being here any longer than he had originally planned and I could hear his hoof tapping impatiently. I remembered the previous arguments of the past where he had fought tooth and hoof to be the main dish. He had even argued about wasting time with Jack and our host.

In studying Ralph, I could see the small sweat dripping down his forehead as more ooze came out of his horn. I could feel the pain now behind the flames in his eyes. He was suffering. The evil darkness in his blood was chewing through his insides like cancer. He was rotting from his insides to his outsides; just like all the other dark unicorns that had sold their souls.

Avaricio smiled wickedly at my wincing sad eyes watching Ralph. Then Avaricio licked the drip down Ralph's long face. Instantly, Ralph's face changed back to a whimsical mean expression and a smile so evil it could curdle dairy.

"Don't worry Ralphie-Boy it will be over before you know it. I will happily have first honors and seconds. I could eat you right now if I had a knife, I am that famished for unicorn meat." Avaricio said as everyone became deathly silent.

Suddenly Avaricio frowned and he let out a pained hiss. Six claw marks suddenly appeared across his shocked face. The cuts had sliced open his pale blue skin. We all knew what had happened but didn't look to see the being who was smiling now.

"Avaricio the tables can turn at any moment from this point on in the game. I would be justified in telling you to keep your tongue and claws off of Ralph. We all have two more hands before anything happens. And in the meantime the Nagas are awakening. Be a dear now and go see if they need anything?" You could hear the smile in my best friend's deep voice which sounded as charming as church bells with a hint of larceny.

His voice carried through what remained of the cave walls and cheerfully rang with the world clock that chimed midnight. I held my breath as Avaricio stood up folding his new hand immediately and we were all dealt another new hand instantly. As he walked away from the table his chair disappeared and the table magically changed into a smaller form.

Avaricio barely made it down the stairs into the bleakness of the underbelly of the cave before we heard his screams and then an eerie silence. The archangel that had been silently watching Avaricio closed his eyes in saying an inaudible afterlife chant that sounded like a song for the recently departed. Then the silence became deafening.

"Good, now that the Nagas are partially fed we can continue. That sin should not have been so." He smiled at his riddle and I smiled back at his poetic beauty and the fact he had stuck up for Ralph.

Luxuria was red faced and her tears were flowing. I was shocked by this display of emotion from her. She had been a proud dark elven warrior before her misuse of power. But maybe the reality of the situation we were in was finally dawning on her.

All of us had been here by choice but now I was thinking maybe she wasn't.

🌱🌱🌱

CHAPTER 8

LUXURIA

"Focus on the game Luxuria. Instead of showing off your delights and then maybe you could play better. But I am sure that won't help your situation either." The Morning Star spoke bright but Luxuria instantly winced in a wounded expression as if his voice was inflicting some invisible sting at her.

She defiantly stood up and took off her black hooded sweatshirt and pants. But no one seemed to care. Jack and I folded immediately as we watched the secret masters of our universe actually playing some game between themselves with only a few bystanders hanging in to spectate.

I heard a huge sigh in frustration as Ralph's black onyx hair seemed to be falling out so much that he tried to gather the remnants off the table. Luxuria's pretty face scrunched up in disgust as Ralph tried to scoop up the golden glitter that seemed to separate from the black tar of his blood.

"Can it be done Morning Star? Please, I don't think I can take the aching anymore." Ralph said as his voice cracked.

"We still have another hand Ralph. Please drink your tea my guests and none of you shall feel pain ever again." The sound of his deep voice was hypnotic and soothed me completely.

Even though I was shocked by the teacups suddenly appearing with pink liquid in them; I was more mesmerized by my best friend's whole physical being. He gave me a wink as I downed my cup immediately. He had caught me starring at him and I could feel the heat in my cheeks as I drank my delicious strawberry tea.

We all obeyed without question because we all knew this pink bubble tea was a kindness that would never be offered to any of the other souls he would pillage later in the early morning. I watched as the exquisite archangel stood up and took his scythe. His black cloak cascaded around his black glowing feathered wings which now radiated with the same golden shimmering light which cascaded our loving host.

"Dear guests I have to go. A smaller meteor has touched down and now a tsunami is racing towards Hawaii. The surrounding islands will be submerged in minutes. Thank you for letting me sit with you all. Be merry and I will see you all very soon. Thank you for this game Morning Star. See you later Alligator."

"After while Crocodile." Morning Star said very deep and straight faced and then they both burst into laughter.

"Oh you kill me." Morning Star said so brightly.

"Soon my friend; very soon." Then they both paused and laughed again before Azrael left on a mysterious white Pegasus that seemed to appear by the stairs.

He took off through the giant hole where the ceiling used to be.

Just then I glanced over to Luxuria who had this murderous expression now on her face. She hadn't even picked up her teacup.

Ralph and Jack seemed to notice this at the same time as I did. They couldn't hide their shocked expressions as Ralph pushed the small tea cup towards Luxuria with his bloody hoof.

"You are such a fool. Do you think you can actually tempt me? You are no more than a glorified stable horse; too broken to ride and overdue for the glue factory." She shouted as she pulled out her dagger from her boot and slammed it down on the table in front of her.

"Listen Lady, I know who you are and I don't care. Drink that pink bubble tea and you won't feel the taste of death's scythe. You heard what he said. We are all not above him or God. The house always wins lady or maybe you have more breasts than brains." Ralph looked like he was exhausted by just speaking to her, but then his cheeks became rosy.

Suddenly his whole disposition changed and he became merrier by the minute. He was now actually happy. We all were.

"This is poison you idiot. I think the only one of you that has a brain in there head is Thomas. And it's only because he's been quiet this whole time." Luxuria shouted and spit when she spoke.

"We all know this." Ralph said and laughed with Jack.

"Why would you choose to drink it then?" Luxuria held her dagger to Ralph's throat but he just laughed in her face.

"We chose to be here. Not to seduce anyone; and not to fight anyone. I have done many dark things in my lifetimes Luxuria; all of which I regret now. But being here and giving my life force has never been a regret for me. As soon as you crossed the threshold of the temple's cave entrance you were cursed. There are many deaths that can occur deep inside these walls regardless if the magic temple of the cave even collapses. Drink the tea Luxuria and liberate your soul." Ralph said and Jack and I nodded in agreement.

"I am not dying here. I will fight anyone who lays a hand on me." Luxuria shouted but removed her blade from Ralph's neck.

Ralph was still smiling even though everyone grew quiet at seeing the slight glittered-tar ooze from the small cut now across his neck.

"Why fight your destiny Luxuria? Go with honor and return home to the magic." Ralph said in a soothing tone that I had never heard before.

"Ralph she doesn't understand the agreement her and Avaricio made as soon as she sat at the table. No matter how much you try to reason with the dammed; you cannot make anyone drink the tea of truth. Free will was given to all." My best friend's voice was deep but gentle as he spoke to Ralph and I noticed his little teacup was empty too.

"Yes my Prince, I understand now. Thank you for this divine gift. I feel so good. I feel like I could grow wings and fart rainbows." Ralph said and chuckled as we laughed with him.

Luxuria wasn't laughing. Her cheeks were a darker shade of red now. But I didn't care about anything. I felt like a million bucks and Jack's once worried expression seemed to be long gone. We were all dealt a new hand while all the teacups disappeared. We started lively talking before the next game started. A little cart appeared in arm's reach of Jack filled with all different fairy cakes and strawberry custard parfaits. It was a glorious batch of desserts including the wonderful cookies layered on the Ark of the Covenants golden lid.

"This is the best Morning Star." I said and he winked again to me as he ate another gourmet donut from the ones I had brought earlier.

"Shut up everyone and start playing. All of you could do well to stop eating so much, especially you Ralph." She shouted as Ralph continued to eat a giant piece of custard filled cake.

Ralph looked at her and then looked at us; we all laughed and laughed hysterically. She really didn't know what Ralph was here for. Even Jack and I knew not to question Ralph's indulgence. Thomas was quiet but smiling as he ate his chocolate cupcake with his green top hat next to him on his chair.

The only one who wasn't having fun and enjoying themselves was Luxuria. She was wearing what looked like the skimpiest of leather bikini tops and no one was paying attention. She seemed flawless except the scowl on her face. We were joking and eating so much that the game had actually stopped and the cards and chips had disappeared.

Then the world clock chimed at Twelve forty-five in the morning; like it had some kind of magical alarm button giving us a warning. With a wave of my best friend's hand, the table cloth was now cleared. The chips were restacked neatly and the food had disappeared. I gently touched my best friends arm and he grabbed my hand and kissed it tenderly as everyone's cards were dealt.

The floating score card suddenly appeared with Avaricio's name scratched out in blood that dripped down to the edge of the board. The score keeping board was quite different from other games. It counted losses over wins because everything was reversed in our game. Ralph was tied with Luxuria in having two losing hands. This revelation made Ralph even happier as he pointed and laughed at Luxuria.

"I'm glad I didn't have to wear a bikini for nothing. It sure was cold in here before I drank that pink brew. Now it is peachy keen and perfectly toasty. I can even here the oven's fire cracking and calling my name. The company and food has been great just like it always is. I gave a five star review before I came." Ralph said and we all laughed with him except Luxuria.

"All in." Ralph said and I cheered him on as his hand was beat by Luxuria and the Morning Star.

I was happy beyond words. I really enjoyed playing cards even though I knew the house always wins. I liked losing. It was more than that. I just loved being in my best friends presence. Jack nudged me again and I quickly folded. I smiled at making my best friend blush after daydreaming about him and he caught me again.

"Pay attention Julia. You're such an ugly hag. I don't even know why you are here. You are the most pathetic excuse for a human being I have ever met. Human…more like freak." Luxuria snapped and kicked me hard under the table with her spiked boots.

I didn't feel any pain and laughed hard. The others laughed with me as Luxuria gave murderous looks to us all. When Jack laughed he pointed to the blood soaking through the bottom of my indigo striped grecian dress and it made me giggle harder. But quicker than we all could speak my best friend snapped his fingers and Luxuria had deep claw marks across her chest. Her cuts oozed a black-purplish blood. Then we saw the trickle of blood from a separate gash on her neck that just appeared.

"Blood for blood Luxuria, isn't that the way of your proud elvish warrior bloodline?" His stern deep voice was now eerie.

"Yes." Luxuria whimpered as tears trickled out of her eyes.

She sat there still sticking her chin out in defiance but it was plain to see she was suffering as her tears flowed.

"Please my dearest friend, I have never felt better thanks to you. This is a lovely time of serenity between beloved old-time friends. Do not let my injury ruin our needed amusement." I said as I placed my hand gently on his muscular forearm and he took my hand and kissed his ring he had given me.

"For you my love, I would rearrange the stars so they would shine brighter every time you spoke. I would enchant every flower to bloom more joyfully in your presence. I would even place every one of Luxuria's ancestors in a barbeque and serve them on a silver platter for a mere hint of your affection." He cooed to me and I almost fainted.

"You are so magmatic and kind your highness. But all I want is you beside me in my darkest of hours, which you are. How could I ask for anything more my immortal love?" My smile was even warmer as I cherished him calling me *his love* and kissed him devotedly.

"My sweet little Flame, your heart is glowing." His deep whisper sent shivers down my spine of pure ecstasy.

I blushed and then he leaned over and kissed me even more passionately. I swear I was swooning even by the twinkle in his ocean blue eyes for me. Instantly, a teacup appeared in front of Luxuria with the same magic pink bubble tea that everyone had drank before.

"I suggest you drink this time and finish it. You won't get another opportunity to experience such kindness from me in this lifetime and in future lifetimes." His voice sounded sultry and sinister as he glared at her.

Luxuria broke out in goosebumps across her arms and chest.

"I would rather suffer than let one human have the satisfaction of being the one who brought true love and bliss; to the Prince of Darkness. I should be the one. It should be me, not you Julia. You can shove that tea up your unholy ass." Luxuria shouted as she stood up suddenly and threw the teacup in my face.

But the tea and cup disappeared before it hit my smiling face. Then we looked down and noticed the cards were all face up and Luxuria's chips were all in; beside Ralph's chips and the Morning Star's chips. The rest of us gasped but held smiles on our faces. Ralph started laughing and we all joined in; the pink tea made everything funny even when it wasn't.

Luxuria had a bad beat. She had a full house with threes over sixes. Ralph had a full house as well, with sixes over kings. But the Morning Star had a blood red royal flush. His fanged grin grew maliciously as he picked up his cards to show us the dripping hearts on his cards. I gently congratulated him by patting and kissing his hand.

Luxuria's face went a shade of gray I had never witnessed on any creature that was suddenly struck with some invisible plague. Suddenly the music started playing louder from the radio in the darkness. The radio had tuned to a station where a fun upbeat nineties pop song played and it was as if someone had cranked it opportunistically.

Then I watched as Luxuria's eyes went wide. We watched and we sang in our uncontrolled happiness as the shadow people were taking her. Their hands and arms were everywhere restraining her before she could even fight back. One held her mouth open as another took giant shears and chopped off her tongue. Tears were streaming as she tried to unsuccessfully wrestle to break free, even with black-purple blood oozing out of her mouth and dripping down her chin.

Then just like that she was being dragged away into the darkness. But we saw one last parting image as she was dragged through a doorway that magically opened from a slice through the fabric of reality. All you could see was the great red dragon's mouth she was being dragged to. She was then striped and we saw the scythe swing removing her head with a sickening thud just before the doorway shut. Reality returned back to the crystal glowing lights of the partial cave wall.

The radio uplifted all of our already happy moods as we noticed Luxuria's chair was now gone and any other remnant of her even being there. The score board had even scratched out her name so much it was indistinguishable from the bloody line across it.

The pink potion was amazing for a simple tea. It took away any pain; intoxicating all who drank it into pure unrelenting happiness. I could have and hold the knowledge of dread of what had happened to Luxuria. But I was deliriously happy instead. I even joined in singing the next pop song on the radio. Jack and Ralph had joined in singing too. Ralph who normally wore a permanent frown was bursting with happiness. I wondered if they had felt bad for Luxuria.

I knew one other thing about myself in this moment of shock on the inside and happiness on the outside; I knew secretly a small part of me was even happier she was gone. I could hold the knowledge of the hate and jealously I had felt when she took off her sweater and when she mocked my best friend. Secretly I was glad she got what she deserved for being so defiant. I also knew I wasn't happy about seeing her purple blood ruin the pretty table cloth; or seeing her unjustified tears. I was more and more happy that she was gone, each time I thought about how vulgar her behavior had been.

But a small part of me also held the knowledge of wishing it didn't have to be that way for her ending. But I was just one human and my heart sung at the knowledge of being the object of my best friend's hungry eyes which were eating me all up. His kisses came just as feverish and I kissed him back just as heated while the song played to our frenzy.

⌾⌾⌾

CHAPTER 9

CELEBRATIONS

With all these thoughts and realizations playing along with the sounds of the radio; I felt even happier as the dessert lid appeared on a magical cart and everyone indulged in more sweets. As the table had shrunk smaller I was now seated across from someone who had been quiet this whole time. I looked across the table at the gentle unobtrusive gentleman who I had completely forgotten about even with his name on the scoreboard after Ralphs.

Thomas had drunk the pink bubble tea with us but had been so silent throughout the game. He had not made a peep of laughter when everyone else had. He had been so quiet like he was almost invisible even in betting and playing cards.

His dark green top hat was now on his head and held a rare orange peacock feather. His cheeks were rosy as he smoked his pipe and stayed still like he was part of the furniture. His suit and vest were that of a bright green shamrock. He looked very gentlemanly. He was another very misunderstood magically creature. He was neither good nor entirely evil as well. He fit right in with us; although in other lifetimes I remember him as being much livelier and much younger.

He smiled warmly at me and I smiled back as I noticed this blue tinge in his kind eyes. Then I realized he had a walking cane beside him.

"Thomas can you see me?" I whispered over to him even as the radio blared.

"I am blind, but I can still see. I can see auras and yours tis' a very pretty green-blue with a hint of gold. My ears have always been sharper even throughout the centuries over ma lost vision." Thomas said politely.

"Thank you Thomas, but what happened to your vision?" I asked and tried to sound polite but wondered if it came across as rude.

"Long ago, before the waters turned to blood, they poisoned the rivers and lakes of the great forests. That was how they wiped us fairies almost off the planet. I can't wait to be finally leaving here. As soon as I cross over I will regain the most precious thing tis' lost to ma soul." Thomas spoke and I watched him close his eyes and smile as if in a sweet dream.

"You will regain your sight back?" I asked with a smile and he looked at me with a grin.

"Yes, but even vision tis' not the most precious thing." Thomas said cheerfully and then I heard the snap.

The table cloth was clear again. The floating scoreboard held Avaricio and Luxuria's names crossed out so violently in dripping lines of crimson scratch marks. Again my brain acknowledged the feeling of dread for what had happened but my face held a wide grin just the same as Jack and Ralph. Thomas held a warm smile but his eyebrows couldn't hold the worry wrinkle creasing his forehead and his little hands resembled ringing out laundry. His hands clasped and held each other for life.

"Thomas are you okay?" The deep voice was gentle and I saw the tenderness in my best friend's enchanting soft blue eyes.

"Yes, but I might need another tea my good friend. I am afraid my magic tis' fighting back the helpful potion and I am feeling things I shouldn't. Tis' a joyful occasion and I am sorry for ruining it." Thomas said as a little tear ran down his rosy cheeks.

"What are you feeling my darling little friend of the woods?"

"My heart tis' hurt from hearing all of the crying and screaming. I can hear millions being tortured beyond the music of the radio. I don't know if I can take their suffering." Thomas said as small tears glistened his cheeks.

"But these are the same humans that have driven you out of your homeland in the ancient forests." Our host spoke gracious with so much compassion my heart sighed.

"Be it truth you speak. I know it in the sadness of my heart. But the humans that found me saved ma life and tried to heal ma village. Tis' not all humans that killed the leprechauns; just like tis' not all humans which killed the dragons and unicorns. The world powers that controlled the masses are the true evil ones. But none matters anymore. The anger and rage of my youth were spent a long time ago with needless revenge. All tis' left is an old tired fae living with ghosts and trying to enjoy an exquisite game of cards. There is not one species of being at this table that I consider less than. All of you, I treasure and this ending that my stretched thin bones long for." Thomas spoke softly and eloquently as a few small tears rolled down his cheek.

Instantly another round of tea cups appeared at the table. The pink bubble tea concoction was the same merriment substance. We all toasted each other and chimed our cups before drinking. Thomas thanked our host for being so generous and we all chimed in with thanks.

It seemed to be a small eternity of time of waiting for the cards to be shuffled and a new set of cards being dealt out. Ralph was bursting with happiness even though his ear had fallen off and could not be re-attached; even though I had tried. More and more black-tarred blood oozed out of the hole where his ear used to be. The evil substance resembled molasses slowly dripping onto his shoulder. Because the last hand was ruled void, deemed from excessive cheating from Luxuria; Ralph was all in this round. And Jack, Thomas, and I folded immediately.

Ralph had obeyed the rules and now he was the spoils of a victorious loss. His hand held a pair of threes while our grand Prince of Darkness held another impressive royal flush. Both smiles were contagious as everyone was cheerful.

Ralph would be drained mercifully and then taken away into the darkness where the ovens would blaze for him. In lifetimes before, we all had watched as Ralph sacrificed himself willingly each time and sometimes the darkness would show us how they skinned him and chopped him up. The darkness loved Ralph. It even had a special marinating sauce called; "El King Ralphio." It was a super barbeque sauce to honor Ralph. The darkness had blessed him and all his future ancestries for his service.

But this time while we were playing cards I noticed something. The man in shimmering white robes appeared and the glow of the heavens was through his being. His wingless form was flying through the chaos. He was saving souls and he was directly looking at us. He could see through the cloak of invisibility of our hidden poker game. It was the Chosen One; the Redeemer; and he was now staring at Ralph with such a determined intensity.

My heart was pounding and my brain acknowledged the panicked fear in my heart even though I was still deliriously happy. Just like we all were. Then I noticed the white star on Ralph's chest getting larger. The patch was growing like some kind of invisible dye saturating across his matted black fur. Then in another mere second; the black hooded angel appeared and touched Ralph's shoulder and then was gone just as quickly.

Ralph's eyes were bright and loving. The Morning Star flew over and wrapped Ralph in his giant loving feathers. Ever so gently his fangs enlarged and then sank into Ralph's thick neck. In one motion Ralph was giving us a thumb's up and then in the next moment his arm lay limp.

Ralph's dead stare was still fixed on the man in white; and the man in white was moving even quicker towards us. The shadow people had just raised Ralph's lifeless body and were taking him away when the man in white flew through the giant hole in the cave wall. The Redeemer gently reached into Ralph's lifeless physical body and pulled his soul out.

Ralph's renewed unicorn soul emerged bright, happy, and glorious. Ralph was healed and glowing. He left grinning with the man in white; flying right out of the cave and up towards the heaven; and way passed our view.

"Woah, did Ralph just get saved?" Jack whispered to me and I shrugged.

"I don't think it's possible." I whispered back.

We all watched Ralph's physical shell of a body vanish into the darkness. Then seconds later we could smell the roast coming from the ovens. Ralph smelt like the best barbequed meat in existence. I noticed Jack stick his nose in the air sniffing the glorious culinary delight of our unicorn friend.

🌾🌾🌾🌾

CHAPTER 10

RALPHS VICTORY

"To answer your question; yes even you can be saved. It has never been Ralph's soul that the darkness needed. It has always been his meat. The Redeemer and Champion of Light, is harvesting souls right now too. Just because you have feasted with me does not limit you to being rescued in the final hours." Our magmatic host spoke deep but gentle and I suddenly realized the table had become much smaller.

Instinctively, I reached out and was touching his soft but firm arm. His skin had become even more electric to the touch as his angelic soul was ramping up for war. He was smiling with us but I wondered if he felt my thoughts of missing Ralph.

"Yes Julia, I will miss Ralph just like I will miss you all. I don't know if this is the final game or not. All of you have a chance to get out of this contract still. Nothing is ever certain in this life except our dark hooded friend from earlier that works for the Great Creator." He said as smooth as silk and I felt my breath get caught in my throat.

The mood at the table seemed to shift. I think everyone was thinking what I was unexpectedly feeling. *What do you mean?*

"I can't. I need that sense of purpose. I need that afterlife-service job I provide with the pack. It's the only thing I look forward to after facing each agony of all the full moons of my life. That and being with Julia through all the realms." Jack said as he smiled but I caught the panic in his tone.

"But I have noticed the white patch on your fur in the shape of the star. And now your hair has turned golden Jack. What have you done this time that was different?" The Morning Star's voice was deep but patient as cards were shuffled.

"Julia and I saved the children in the woods."

"Jack, we have done that before." I said and tried to ease both our involvements.

"This is the same children you have sought out revenge for in all your past lives. Haven't you ravaged and torn apart the children's captors?" Our host's deep voice was still patient as the cards were being shuffled.

"Usually, we have always done this. But this time was different. Julia and I hunted down the group and were going to get revenge when the man in white appeared. The Redeemer told us there was another way. He told me he would take care of the evil people if I just surrendered justice and their fate to him. With all my built up anger from my robbed childhood and everything cruel that has ever happened to me in my life for being born this tortured creature; I started to rage wanting blood. Julia had my back and was following my actions when the man in white touched both our arms. Then we left the area immediately." Jack said and looked at me and I nodded and looked down.

"What? What happened? Did Jesus the Destroyer hurt you both?"

"No, actually it was the opposite. I felt this immense supernatural love I have never experienced before; and it was all from his touch." Jack said and quickly turned his eyes to his new cards.

"The mere touch of his hand transformed my feelings to peace and love in my soul. I finally felt like I belonged to something greater and so I just left with Julia. The Redeemer disappeared shortly after." Jack said and then traded out two cards; then Thomas went all in.

"But those bad people; what happened to them?" Thomas asked politely but held a worried look.

"It turns out the military was hunting me and Julia. When I had found that despicable group of child murderers; the government had too and they let us go because we were no longer the greatest threat. Then the government was merciless and far more evil in their punishments than what we were going to do." Jack said while looking at me and I nodded; it was all true.

It was the first time in a long time I seen the centuries of sadness in Jacks eyes.

Then we watched as the Ark of the Covenant's lid which had previously held desserts; now held a decorated platter of roasted, coal-like meat. There were also hooves decorated with flowers in the center. There were platters and platters of meat being whisked by us down into the darkness where we could hear these magical popping sounds. All the Nagas were completely transforming back to angels.

"Ralph is ready my guests. Please enjoy yourselves and dig in." The Morning Star said and gave a look of being famished as his fangs elongated even more.

"Please forgive me your highness; I have lost my appetite." Jack said and I patted his arm knowing when he was in human form he was a vegetarian.

"You must try some of our good friend as it was his dying request. We need to honor his sacrifice and wishes. Without Ralph's willing sacrifice all of you would have been on the menu and many more." Our gracious host said and his deep gentle voice gave me small goosebumps in knowing what he was saying was true.

He only spoke the truth.

It was our job to honor Ralph but in all my past lives this is what my soul dreaded. I knew Jack felt the same way. I was having déjà vu and remembered this horrific scene just like what I was seeing today and my stomach was turning.

Each of us took a small piece of black glittering meat and chewed. The barbeque sauce was thick but my tears were thicker as my best friend ate the horn like candy. Then as quick as the teacups appeared we all drank the pink concoction again.

☘☘☘☘

CHAPTER 11

SIMPLE THOMAS AND SWEET JACK

Thomas lay there with a smile on his face and simply closed his eyes as the color faded from his once rosy cheeks. In one flash our black cloaked friend swooped down and touched Thomas' hand and then was gone. The strong arms that were holding him gently placed him down as the shadow people took away his empty physical body. We sat there in strange aw as the spirit of Thomas floated up and stood facing the broken wall.

Suddenly a doorway opened up through the fabric of time to another galaxy. We watched Thomas skipping and dancing through the sunshine filled meadow where he was greeted by his family and friends. They swarmed him in a community embrace. Then I noticed the world clock as the portal was closing and we were waving goodbye to Thomas.

The clock had been ticking away this whole time and the last few hands of cards were a frenzied fuzziness folding so certain members of our friend group could get their turn to end their game. All of us wanted the same thing. All of our souls were tired and couldn't wait for the other realm of fun. This world had been hard and over time had got even harder. *Where was humanity going? Would there be another reset? Would get to play again or was this it?* These thoughts stirred my soul and Jack turned to hug me tight.

Then the hands of the clock froze on a quarter to three. In the same flash I saw the scythe of our angel friend once more as he touched my hand and Jacks. Then the black cloaked angel was gone a second later.

"I'm sorry my two lovelies. We never got to finish the game. But you both are tied for second place. My dear sweet Jack, please come to me now. We can all watch the rest of the angels leave the cave in a glowing fury before the even greater meteor hurtles towards us. But you both must be gone before the meteor touches down. I need to be out harvesting souls soon." His voice still loving held a stern urgency.

"Yes my magnificent Prince." Jack said as we both stood up and walked towards the golden throne while the table disappeared.

"Hey Julia, see you soon on the other side hopefully." Jack said as a joke but it raised alarms inside my gut.

"What do you mean? We always end up together." I said while hugging him as he hugged me tighter.

My tears held back in the corners of my eyes as he whispered he loved me and I mouthed the words back to him.

"Remember death is only the beginning. I will find you like I always do and I will help you protect the children like we always do." I said and kissed his cheek.

"Yes, maybe you could fly us again to another area like before." Jack said as he turned to be embraced by the Morning Star's great arms.

His giant black wings covered Jack like a blanket full of soft clouds and Jack was still smiling as he gave me a peace sign. Then the gentle cotton of his jogging suit made a ruffled soft sound as more shadow people took his physical body away.

It was at this moment that the giant cave doors of the temple were blasted away and the light of all the fires and a sea of red were visible. I watched as the beautiful fallen angels flew out into the even more imminent darkness of screams and chaos.

When I turned back I was just able to see the Redeemer take Jacks smiling floating spirit to float through a sunny portal door where the other lycans were pushing a group of children on swings. He was greeted by our wolf pack as soon as he crossed through the gateway.

I giggled as I heard them call out to Jack to see if this time he could hold his plasma as they dared him to go on the cursed merry-go-round. He turned back just before the portal closed.

"Hey Julia, I love you my mate and my best friend. No matter where you go in the universe I want you to know; I have always loved you my best friend in obsolete time and forever space." Jack said and waved goodbye to me and then the gateway vanished.

≱≱≱≱

CHAPTER 12

FAREWELL LOVE

"Wait, what did Jack mean by *if* he got to see me again?" I said and was suddenly panicked like if someone just took the teddy bear I had held through all lifetimes.

I tried to recall there ever being sunshine in the realm of the in-between where we were the guardians. It suddenly hit me and I felt like vomiting. *It has always been a world without the sun. I saw the crystal blue sky and seen the richest grass and most vibrant colors that I have ever seen in my life. Something is different. Where did Jack go?*

"You are correct my love. Jack changed his timeline and now he is in his version of heaven with the others who are now serving the light." His deep voice was sweet as he caressed my face.

"But how can this be?" I whispered but did not need an answer as I knew it was the man in white.

The Redeemer had saved everyone who had accepted him. All he had to do was touch you and you had been saved. The creatures born into darkness were no exception. My mind raced as I tried to piece the puzzle together and felt even more nauseous. A hopelessness started to sweep through my body. *My Love what does this mean?*

"This time is the end. But I'm not one hundred percent sure because the orders have not come yet from above. Your souls have served and fulfilled their purpose for the balance to be restored in the Universe. Your contract is fulfilled as soon as I drink from you and let you go. Julia there is no need for you to follow me across the galaxy to the abyss of final darkness. I am the Prince but you are human. Even my powers cannot stop the everlasting fire that awaits you; if you join me. You know it is time. You have to call upon Jesus the Destroyer of Darkness. Say his name or think his name and he shall appear; and then you shall be brought to the sun-filled realm with Jack. You are saved from this peril." His deep voice was sorrowful as he brought me to sit on his lap and whispered as a lover to my beating heart.

He gave me another pink tea and drank one with me; toasting to everlasting happiness. But my tears were streaming down my face.

"This means we won't be able to be together…for the rest of eternity." I felt my breath stop as the words passed on my lips penetrating my soul in a deathly wound.

I started crying and held him tighter. I kissed him long and true but when I opened my eyes I seen his cold golden eyes looking back at me. He had a duty that he was being called upon and I was delaying his importance to the universal plan.

"I don't think I can leave you. I love you too much." I whispered as I tried to touch his face but he gently grabbed my hand and stopped me.

"But you have already left me. Do you remember before I came to you in your dreams? Do you remember in college when you went to that camping trip in Lake St. Peter? There was a massive baptism that day and the whole lake was blessed. You were already tainted then. That was why I was so unhinged when I first saw your face in the library. I had seen the invisible mark on your forehead and it stung my eyes. Yet I still pursued you, knowing you would break my heart." His grave voice pierced my heart in that moment.

"But baptism doesn't mean anything does it?" I asked in a hush because I knew the answer. My soul knew.

"It does when you and Jack decided to not get revenge that day. You chose different paths that day and left me. And then you silently made a prayer for Ralph to have his suffering end." He whispered in his strong deep voice and I felt a lump get stuck in my throat.

"But..."

"In praying, you believe in the light and the higher being of love. You believe in the Divine so greatly that the magic of the light had come through and took Ralph out of the darkness." His voice seemed colder and distant even as my tears came down.

"I need you though. I need your touch...your love. I need your heavy beating heart against mine. I don't know how I can live an eternity without you. I love you." I whispered in a panic as I clung to him.

"You must Julia. You must. I am going to a place where I couldn't stand to see you in a cage or the flaming pit. You forget I am a Prince and my first duty is for the King's contentment. What we have has always been a beauty I had never thought I would ever know. In all my lifetimes the love you have given me has helped me succeed in battle. I am grateful for the eons of love and earthly pleasure you have brought me. You have brought the damn sunshine to my eternal darkness and I am deeply moved by your heart. But I need to focus and obey the orders given to me by the most Highest Divine and you need to leave right now. You have to go to a place where I know you will be safe. You need to forget our love. You need to forget me. The only reason I never slayed Jack was because I knew with him you were safe. He could give you the free love I never was allowed to. You need to be safe. Call upon the Redeemer now." His voice was dark and deeper but I was still unravelling and completely trying to cling to us.

I needed any last fragment of hope that we could still be together and that he wasn't saying goodbye.

"Safe from whom? You are more powerful than anything I have ever known. You are my everything. Why can't we be together in the darkness?"

"You lie. I know when the Redeemer touched your arm you felt the power. Stop this now. We can't be together. It has always been forbidden Julia. And even now I can see the light bursting through you soul trying to surround your defiance. You have left me and now I am leaving you. Call upon The Destroyer or I shall never kiss you again in any lifetime of realms." His deep chilling voice sent shivers down my spine.

I cried and silently called for the Redeemer to come and save me. My beautiful Morning Star held me tight in his strong arms and kissed me while his soft feathers cuddled my skin. He kissed me down to my neck and then sank his fangs in but all I felt was love and the power in his grace. His soft gentle feathers touched my skin as I hugged him until my physical strength left my body.

My spirit floated out of my body in happiness and then I saw the Redeemer greeting me with open arms. As I started to float away uncontrollably to the portal of light I turned back to see my best friend holding and weeping over me. He had kissed my face as he sobbed still clinging to my limp body. His wet eyes were kissing my cheeks and mouth over and over.

I reached down and gently kissed his golden locks. He suddenly locked eyes with mine and tried to kiss my cheek that was now just a wisp. His eyes glowed as he stood up looking to my spirit floating away uncontrollably.

"I will find you again. I promise. The next time we will have more time my Love. If we get another chance, I shall find you even if it is in this world or the next. We shall have our heavenly love. I promise you I shall find you." He shouted to me and I tried to reach for his hand that tried to grab mine but the vortex of light was stronger.

I was rushed through the portal gateway of light just as a giant meteor crashed down.

🌾🌾🌾🌾

♠The End♠

EPILOGUE

AFTERLIFE AND IN-BETWEEN

Space is timeless. My weeping soul was now adjusting to my new afterlife of service. I was thrust into the realm with the other guardians of light helping the lost souls of children in the in-between of worlds and realms. I had been pushing children on the swings as I looked over to Jack and shook my head as all the children laughed.

Jack was off to the bushes vomiting ecto-plasma from the demonic merry-go-round again. The other werewolves were laughing too as they watched poor Jack, while I walked over to see if he was okay.

"Seriously Jack, I know that you like making the children laugh but there has to be another way. That merry-go-round has the devil in the metal. In that unholy contraption built for fun underlies only fear and nausea." I said to him as he gave me thumbs up and I continued to shake my head; and then smiled as I shrugged in giving up.

This new place was just as peaceful as the other realm had been from all the other lifetimes of servitude. But this place was sunny unlike the darkness realm I usually ended up with Jack. It really was a beautiful afterworld and I had a job of service that I enjoyed; even if it was kind of a glorified babysitting gig in the afterlife.

I continued to pat Jack's back as he heaved.

"Seriously, I'm fine. I can't believe that cursed merry-go-round is here." Jack said as he wiped his mouth and smiled.

"Well the children love it and they always love it when you lose your plasma all over that rose bush." I said and laughed and Jack laughed too.

He was already up and ready to go back to the steel bars. He started running faster pushing the bars for the kids cheering him on. Jack was a favorite guardian of the children. I think they saw him as a giant teddy bear that told funny jokes and farted a lot; and not at all like the fierce guardian warrior he had become. All the guardians had gone through fierce warrior training, including myself. But even with spirits and angels coming and going; this place was very uplifting and fun.

All of a sudden a portal opened up like a tear in reality of existence. A large, dark cloaked figure flew through the hole and their golden wings spread wide. My gaze followed the figure as they stood at a distance from us at first and the golden radiance shimmered even in the daylight.

Beings were always coming and going in this space but this figure seemed brighter than any of the other beings that had ever arrived. There was this golden radiance coming from the being's chest. The being was glowing even with their hood up and their face covered. I immediately started to fly over and started to greet this new being in welcome to this peaceful space.

Before I could speak the being slowly pulled down the dark hood of their cloak revealing a large glittering golden crown. I became speechless as my tears welled. Suddenly they opened their strong arms and I rushed towards them.

He immediately held me tight wrapping his soft golden wings gently around me in a blanket. He kissed me deeply. Then he cupped my face gazing his golden eyes into mine with such longing. A few of his droplets glistened onto my already wet cheeks. Only for one moment he grabbed my hand and slipped his ring back on my finger. Then as he kissed my face over and over; he paused as he gently cupped my face in his gently but firm hands. His voice deep and now golden as he spoke my heart leaped for joy and swooned in his deep loving blue gaze.

"My love I finally found you."

🌾🌾🌾🌾

Some say true love finds us in any lifetime in any galaxy. True love cannot be stopped even in the very end of the fabric of the Ether. True love truly transcends time and space and last for all of eternity.

🌾🌾🌾🌾

ACKNOWLEDGMENTS

I would really like to express my sincere gratitude to; The Universe, my fans, family, and friends. Its fine people like you that give struggling authors a chance. Thank you again!

I would also like to thank my mechanics and my friends Eric Heldman and Jay Flowers at Cormier's Good Year Obsentia, in Quinte West, Ontario. Thank you for always being great friends and taking care of my car. I am so appreciative that you are lights in the world and practice random acts of kindness every day. Thank you again for not suing me for killing off your characters in future novels! Their website is here if you want some kind individuals helping you with your auto needs and are in the Quinte West Area: https://www.trentontire.ca/

Thank you for reading!   I really hope you have liked my book. Please add a short review and let me know what you thought!

And always let your light shine bright!

ABOUT THE AUTHOR

A.L. Secord is a pen name for the author APRIL SECORD. She enjoys many genres. But she is most passionate about Dark Fantasy Romance. She loves learning new things, and occasionally burning food for the ones she loves. She is an author, a proud mother, and an avid adventurer of the unknown; on her many pursuits for greater happiness and Bigfoot.

A CHRISTMAS DARK FANTASY ROMANCE

FOREST LOVE

BROKEN VAMPIRE PRINCE

A.L. SECORD

A DARK FANTASY ANTI-HERO ROMANCE NOVEL

THE LAST KING

EVIL TASTES GOOD

A.L. SECORD

Enjoy other books by
A.L. SECORD: